50 WORLD-RECORD WRITING PROMPTS

Super-Motivating, Reproducible Prompts That Use Amazing World Records as Springboards to Great Writing

Justin McCory Martin

SCHOLASTIC
PROFESSIONAL BOOKS

NEW YORK · TORONTO · LONDON · AUCKLAND · SYDNEY

NEW DELHI · MEXICO CITY · HONG KONG · BUENOS AIRES

To Andrew Martin—
who holds a world's record
for being the best brother

Cover design by James Sarfati
Interior design by Grafica, Inc.
Illustrations by Mike Moran
ISBN: 0-439-29466-5

Table of Contents

Introduction 4

Prompts

Speedy Tale 5

Bedtime Story 6

Green Eggs and Yams 7

A Fifth Face on Rushmore 8

If This Tree Could Talk... 9

The Mall with It All 10

Bird-Brained Story 11

Small World 12

A Scoop of History 13

Backtrack 14

A Bicycle Built for 200 Million 15

For Your Own Amusement 16

Peanut Butter Barn 17

Cyber Fan Letter 18

Personal Favorite 19

Rhode Island Getaway 20

Memory Stretcher 21

The One-Hour President 22

Norilsk Forecast 23

My Movie 24

Flight 1784 to Katmandu 25

Tall Tale 26

Bonjour From Paris 27

Strength or Speed? 28

Rub-a-Dub-Dub, 75 Snakes in a Tub 29

Home Sweet Pumpkin 30

Smart Gadget 31

"Thanks. Now, Where Do We Put This?" .. 32

Collectors' Corner 33

Adventure on the Nile 34

Fantasy Fan Club 35

Zero Stars, Down, an F Minus 36

Schoolhouse Rap 37

"Now I've Seen It All!" 38

Hype-r-text 39

Thar She Blows! 40

The Cheetah and the Sloth 41

On the Cover of Super Star 42

Go for the Gold 43

Virginia Is for Presidents 44

RoboVacuum 45

Fun with Tunnels 46

Natural Wonder Land 47

The Quick and the Odd 48

Adventures of Ultra-Stretch Man
and Elasto-Woman 49

MyLife.com 50

CoolSoft. 2.0 51

Hamlet the Traveling Cat 52

Chilly Inn 53

World's Silliest Record 54

World Record Writing Paper 55

Introduction

Kids love to write … once they get started. Often all they need is a bit of inspiration. Here they'll get inspiration by the bucketful. The prompts contained in this book are based on world records—some strange, some fascinating, all thought-provoking. This is the kind of stuff that can really fire up the imagination, turning even the most reluctant student into an enthusiastic writer.

The prompts in this book are based on everything from the sloth (world's slowest mammal) to the Millennium Force (world's fastest roller coaster). There are also prompts related to young inventors, age-old redwood trees, Olympic medallists, box-office bombs, the biggest, the smallest, the longest, the smartest, and the weirdest.

This book provides kids with a variety of exercises, everything from writing a postcard from Paris to selecting a fifth face to appear on Mount Rushmore. Kids also are challenged to create advertisements, rap songs, bedtime stories, e-mails, and a variety of other written forms.

Your students may get so carried away that they run out of writing room. If so, not to worry. Simply photocopy and provide the additional paper found on page 55. And by all means, encourage your students to share their written work. Of course, you also can have your students respond to the prompts by typing on a computer. That opens up all kinds of fun possibilities, such as creating a booklet composed of the students' work. There's plenty of flexibility in how these exercises can be used. And they certainly will help kids become improved writers who are better prepared for various standardized tests and assessments.

Most of all, enjoy! Here's hoping this book helps your students enjoy writing in a way that's, well, worthy of a world record.

Speedy Tale ☆

The world's fastest animal is the peregrine falcon. It can fly up to 175 miles per hour. That's faster than a NASCAR driver! Now, how about doing some high-speed writing. Take five minutes to fill this entire page with a fun and fast story. On your mark, get set, go!

_____

_____

_____

_____

_____

_____

_____

_____

_____

_____

_____

_____

_____

_____

_____

Bedtime Story ☆

oala bears sleep more than any other animal in the world. There are 24 hours in a day, and they spend 22 of them snoozing. These strange Australian critters are nocturnal, meaning the short time they're awake is actually during the night. They spend that time munching on eucalyptus leaves. Visit the library or use the internet to research facts about koala bears. Then write a bedtime story that includes at least three facts about koalas.

_____

_____

_____

_____

_____

_____

_____

_____

_____

_____

_____

_____

_____

_____

Green Eggs and Yams

The yam is the world's largest vegetable. The biggest yams on record are nearly 10 feet long and weigh roughly 150 pounds. When it comes to vegetables, yam is a fun name to say, too. It rhymes with all kinds of words: "wham," "ham," "ram," and "Uncle Sam." Write a Dr. Seuss-style story about a yam. This will help you get started: **I am who I am. I just bought a big yam!**

_____

_____

_____

_____

_____

_____

_____

_____

_____

_____

_____

_____

_____

_____

_____

A Fifth Face on Rushmore

Mount Rushmore in South Dakota features the faces of four U.S. presidents: George Washington, Thomas Jefferson, Abraham Lincoln, and Theodore Roosevelt. The faces are 60 feet high, making them the world's largest portrait busts. What if you could add a fifth face to Mount Rushmore? It doesn't have to be a president—it can be a sports hero, a doctor, or even your next door neighbor. Now, write about who you would choose for Mount Rushmore and describe why this person is important to you.

_____

_____

_____

_____

_____

_____

_____

_____

_____

_____

_____

_____

_____

_____

_____

If This Tree Could Talk ...

There's a redwood tree in California that is believed to be 12,000 years old. Incredible! America has only been a nation for a little more than 200 years. The pyramids in Egypt are 3,000 years old. Think about all the things that have happened while this tree has been alive. If this tree could talk, what do you think it would say? Stretch your imagination by writing a monologue. A monologue is a long speech made by one person—or in this case, by a tree. Imagine that you are the famous California redwood, the world's oldest living creature, and write a monologue about all the things you've seen over the years.

_____

_____

_____

_____

_____

_____

_____

_____

_____

_____

_____

_____

_____

_____

The Mall with It All

The world's largest mall is in Alberta, Canada. It's called the West Edmonton Mall, and it has 800 stores, 26 movie theaters, an amusement park, and even dolphin shows. Imagine that an even larger mall was built in your town. What stores would it have? What restaurants? What kinds of entertainment and unusual attractions? Write about this record-breaking mall, even larger and cooler than the West Edmonton Mall.

_____

_____

_____

_____

_____

_____

_____

_____

_____

_____

_____

_____

_____

_____

_____

Bird-Brained Story

An African gray parrot named Alex holds the world record for most words learned. He knows more than 80! Pretend you have a pet parrot that knows the following ten words: "carrot," "bird," "yellow," "cold," "happy," "box," "tomorrow," "pizza," "window," and "weird." Give your parrot a name and then write a story that features your talking parrot using the ten words it knows.

_____

_____

_____

_____

_____

_____

_____

_____

_____

_____

_____

_____

_____

_____

_____

_____

Small World ☆

Ever notice how things keep getting smaller and smaller? The world's smallest telephone is just two inches long. The smallest camera is only about an inch wide. How do you feel about things getting smaller? Small stuff is easier to carry, right? But it's easier to lose, too. Do you think there's a way to make teeny tiny cars? Could there be a way to shrink people so they could drive around in these cars? Smallness is kind of a big topic, isn't it? Use your imagination and write about the good and bad sides of things getting smaller.

_____

_____

_____

_____

_____

_____

_____

_____

_____

_____

_____

_____

_____

_____

_____

Name: _____   **Date:** _____

A Scoop of History

The oldest paper in the United States is the Hartford Courant. This Connecticut paper was started in 1764, and it's still around today. Think about all the news stories that have appeared in the Hartford Courant over the years: the elections of every single U.S. president, the beginnings and ends of wars, scientific discoveries, great sporting events, space exploration, you name it. Choose an event from the past. It can be anything, as long as it's interesting and important. Do some research using history books or the internet. Now, write an imaginary Hartford Courant story about the event of your choice. Remember to write a headline.

| Volume XIX | # The Tell-All Tribune | Priceless |

_____

Put your headline here.

_____

_____

_____

_____

_____

Draw a picture to go with your story here.

_____   _____

_____   _____

_____   _____

_____   _____

_____   _____

Backtrack

Arvind Pandya, a man from India, set a world record in 1984 by running backward from Los Angeles to New York. It took him 107 days. Try out a backward exercise of your own. Write your life story in reverse. That means the beginning of your story is something that happened very recently. The end of the story is the day you were born.

_____

_____

_____

_____

_____

_____

_____

_____

_____

_____

_____

_____

_____

_____

_____

_____

A Bicycle Built for 200 Million

The Netherlands is the nation with the most bicycles per capita. It has 16 million of them! That's an average of one bicycle for every citizen, big and small, young and old. Do you think it would be good if people in the United States used bikes and scooters and skateboards more often? What would be the advantages? Would it cut down on pollution? Write about how the United States would be different if people depended on transportation other than cars.

_____

_____

_____

_____

_____

_____

_____

_____

_____

_____

_____

_____

_____

_____

_____

For Your Own Amusement

The Cedar Point amusement park in Sandusky, Ohio, has a roller coaster that holds three world records! The Millennium Force is the world's tallest coaster, standing 310 feet high. It's the fastest, traveling up to 92 miles per hour. And the Millennium Force features the biggest drop: 300 feet straight down! What if you could design your own amusement park? Give it a name and describe the location, the rides, the refreshments, and other fun stuff.

_____

_____

_____

_____

_____

_____

_____

_____

_____

_____

_____

_____

_____

_____

_____

Peanut Butter Barn

The world has more McDonald's than any other restaurant. There are 25,000 McDonald's in 119 different nations. What if you could create your own restaurant chain? What would you serve—pizza, chili, peanut butter sandwiches? Use the space below to write about your restaurant and make sure to include its name, its official colors, advertising slogan, uniforms, and what kind of food you would serve.

_____

_____

_____

_____

_____

_____

_____

_____

_____

_____

_____

_____

_____

_____

_____

_____

_____

_____

Cyber Fan Letter ☆

n 1997, musician Paul McCartney conducted an online chat. He received a record three million e-mails in 30 minutes. Imagine that you could write an e-mail to anyone in the world. Who would it be? What questions would you ask? Use the space below to write an e-mail to the person of your choice.

_____
_____
_____
_____
_____
_____
_____
_____
_____
_____
_____
_____
_____
_____
_____
_____
_____
_____

Personal Favorite

The best-selling album of all time is *Thriller*, by Michael Jackson. It was released in 1982 and has since sold more than 40 million copies. But just because something is the most popular, do you think it's the best? Think about your own personal favorites—in music, movies, food, candy, colors, you name it. Select one that is your favorite, but perhaps not the most popular. For example, maybe you love rhubarb pie, much more than super-popular apple pie. Write about a personal favorite and explain why you like it best.

_____

_____

_____

_____

_____

_____

_____

_____

_____

_____

_____

_____

_____

_____

_____

_____

_____

Rhode Island Getaway

R hode Island is the smallest state in the United States. It's just 48 miles across at its widest point. But it is a very interesting state with a rich history. Visit the library or use the internet to research facts about Rhode Island. Then use the space below to create a mini-report that will make people really want to visit Rhode Island. Make sure to pack in lots of facts—at least ten—about this fascinating little state.

_____

_____

_____

_____

_____

_____

_____

_____

_____

_____

_____

_____

_____

_____

_____

_____

_____

_____

Memory Stretcher

ominic O'Brien from Great Britain has the world's best memory. If he looks just one time at a list of 50 things, he can remember the entire list and repeat it back in perfect order. Now, test your memory. Look out a window for one minute. Then write down everything you remember seeing.

_____

_____

_____

_____

_____

_____

_____

_____

_____

_____

_____

_____

_____

_____

_____

_____

_____

The One-Hour President ☆

Pedro Lascurain served the shortest presidency of any nation ever. He was president of Mexico for just one hour on February 13, 1913, before he resigned. What if you could be president of the United States for just one hour? Would you pass a new law or give a speech? Write about three things you would do during your one hour as president.

_____

_____

_____

_____

_____

_____

_____

_____

_____

_____

_____

_____

_____

_____

_____

_____

Norilsk Forecast

The world's coldest city is Norilsk, Russia. It's home to 170,000 people. But the average temperature is only about 12 degrees Fahrenheit. Pretend you are a TV weather person in Norilsk delivering the forecast. This will help you get started: "Good morning. Today's forecast for Norilsk, very cold. Tomorrow, very cold. Make sure to wear . . ."

_____

_____

_____

_____

_____

_____

_____

_____

_____

_____

_____

_____

_____

_____

My Movie ☆

Tatum O'Neal was the youngest person ever to win an Academy Award. She was just ten years old when she received an Oscar for Best Supporting Actress in 1973 for her performance in the movie *Paper Moon*. What if you were a child movie star? Would you appear in comedies, action films, or serious dramas? Who would be your costars—Jim Carrey, Julia Roberts? Write the story line of an imaginary movie in which you would be the star.

_____

_____

_____

_____

_____

_____

_____

_____

_____

_____

_____

_____

_____

_____

_____

_____

Flight 1784 to Katmandu

The world's busiest airport is Hartsfield International in Atlanta, Georgia. During one year, roughly 73 million travelers pass through this airport! Every day an average of 2,080 planes take off and land here. Think about all the people who pass through this airport. What if you passed through? Where would you be going: to meet long-lost relatives, or on a mountain-climbing adventure in Nepal? Beginning at Hartsfield International Airport, tell the story of a trip you would like to take.

_____
_____
_____
_____
_____
_____
_____
_____
_____
_____
_____
_____
_____
_____
_____

Tall Tale ☆

The world's largest rubberband ball is nearly 13 feet around. It was created by John Bain of Delaware in 1998. The world's tallest candle was 80 feet high. It was made in Sweden in 1897. What if certain smallish things—raindrops, people, grains of rice—got really huge? Let your imagine grow, grow, grow, and write your own tall tale.

_____

_____

_____

_____

_____

_____

_____

_____

_____

_____

_____

_____

_____

_____

_____

_____

_____

_____

Bonjour from Paris

France is the nation that is visited by the most tourists. Roughly 67 million people visit France every year. To learn about France's famous attractions, such as the Eiffel Tower and the Louvre museum, do some research at the library or on the internet. On the front of a card, draw a picture of your favorite sight. On the back, write all about the great places you visited.

GREETINGS FROM FRANCE!

TO:

_____

_____

_____

Strength or Speed?

n 1996 a Belgian man named Walter Arfeuille moved an eight-car train, weighing nearly 500,000 pounds. He was able to pull it more than ten feet … using his teeth. Now that's strong! The world record for high-speed tap dancing belongs to James Devine from Australia. He can tap his feet 38 times per second. Now that's fast! Which would you rather be, strong or fast? Think about it and then write about which one you chose and why.

_____

_____

_____

_____

_____

_____

_____

_____

_____

_____

_____

_____

_____

_____

_____

_____

Rub-a-Dub-Dub, 75 Snakes in a Tub

The world record for the most rattlesnakes in a bathtub with one person is 75. That's right, someone actually sat in a bathtub with 75 poisonous snakes! What do you think: Is it worth it to do something like that simply to set a record? Is sharing a tub with 75 snakes an impressive world record, or is it just plain stupid? Should there be rules preventing people from doing crazy and dangerous things in pursuit of world records?

_____

_____

_____

_____

_____

_____

_____

_____

_____

_____

_____

_____

_____

_____

_____

_____

Home Sweet Pumpkin

Did you know that pumpkins are a kind of fruit? Not only are pumpkins fruit, they're the very largest type. One pumpkin weighed 1,061 pounds. That's a world record! Now, write a fairy tale about a family that lives inside a very large pumpkin.

_____

_____

_____

_____

_____

_____

_____

_____

_____

_____

_____

_____

_____

_____

_____

_____

_____

Smart Gadget

The world's smartest pen can do much more than write. It features a calendar, alarm clock, calculator, and it even receives e-mails. There are lots of smart gadgets available now. Think about a smart gadget you'd like to invent. It can be anything: a smart car or a smart toothbrush. Give your gadget a cool name. Then, create an instruction booklet describing the various things your gadget can do.

Name of gadget here.

Drawing of gadget here.

"Thanks. Now, Where Do We Put This?"

The biggest gift ever is the Statue of Liberty. It was a present from France to the United States in 1886. It stands more than 150 feet tall and weighs 225 tons. What if your town could give a giant gift to another town in the United States or to another country? What would the gift be? For example, if your town is famous for pretzels, maybe you could send a huge iron pretzel to another town. Write about a big gift that your town might give to another town or country and explain why.

_____

_____

_____

_____

_____

_____

_____

_____

_____

_____

_____

_____

_____

_____

_____

_____

_____

_____

Collectors' Corner ☆

The world's largest Barbie collection—1,125 dolls—belongs to Tony Mattia of England. Louise Greenfarb from Spanaway, Washington, has a collection of 29,000 refrigerator magnets, another world record. Do you have a collection of any kind? Is there something that you would like to collect? What would be some of the coolest or rarest items in your collection? Write about a world-record-size collection that you would like to put together.

My Collection

_____

_____

_____

_____

_____

_____

_____

_____

_____

_____

_____

_____

_____

_____

_____

_____

_____

_____

Adventure on the Nile

The Nile is the world's longest river. It flows for 4,145 miles through African nations such as Egypt, Rwanda, and Uganda. Do some research on the Nile at the library or on the internet. Then write a Nile river adventure full of crocodiles and pyramids and whatever else captures your imagination. Be sure to use at least three facts learned during your research.

_____

_____

_____

_____

_____

_____

_____

_____

_____

_____

_____

_____

_____

_____

_____

_____

_____

Fantasy Fan Club ☆

There are 613 Elvis Presley fan clubs. That's a world record! What if you could start a fan club? Who would it be for: a musician, a sports figure, a movie star? Create your own imaginary fan club newsletter. Remember, it has to be full of energy and excitement. This will help you get started: "Guess what? Big news! You'll never believe this …"

FAN CLUB NEWSLETTER FOR

_____

Write name of person here.

BIG NEWS . . .

_____
_____
_____
_____
_____
_____
_____
_____
_____
_____
_____
_____

10 Great Things About _____

Write name of person here.

_____
_____
_____
_____
_____
_____
_____
_____
_____
_____

Draw person here.

THIS JUST IN . . .

_____
_____
_____
_____
_____
_____
_____

Zero Stars, Thumbs Down, an F Minus

Cutthroat Island is the biggest movie flop of all time. It cost $100 million to make and promote. But it only earned $11 million. That means the movie lost $89 million! Basically, people thought this movie was stink-o! Is there a movie that you really hated? Write a bad review of it.

_____

_____

_____

_____

_____

_____

_____

_____

_____

_____

_____

_____

_____

_____

_____

_____

_____

_____

_____

Name: _____ **Date:** _____

Schoolhouse Rap ☆

Chicago's Rebel XD is the fastest rapper in the land. He set a world record in 1992 when he rapped 675 syllables in just under a minute.

That's mighty fast.
Don't come in last.
Make up a rap that steals the show!
Now, write it quickly down below.

_____

_____

_____

_____

_____

_____

_____

_____

_____

_____

_____

_____

_____

_____

_____

_____

_____

"Now I've Seen It All"

Jeanne Louise Calment set the record for living the longest. This French woman lived for 122 years, from February 21, 1875, to August 4, 1997. During her lifetime the world experienced incredible change. She was born during a time of horse-drawn carriages, gas lanterns, and quill pens. By the time she died, the world was full of automobiles, neon lights, and computers. Write about all the amazing changes that might happen if you live to be 122 years old.

_____

_____

_____

_____

_____

_____

_____

_____

_____

_____

_____

_____

_____

_____

_____

_____

Hype-r-text ☆

Coca-Cola is the most popular soft drink of all time. It was invented in Atlanta in 1886 by a pharmacist named John Stith Pemberton. These days people around the world drink nearly 700 million Cokes every single day! Think about a product you would like to invent. Would it be a type of drink, perhaps, or a toy? Use the space below to create an advertisement for your product. Describe it carefully and in a fun way. And don't forget to include a great picture. Remember, you want lots of people to buy your product so that it will be as popular as Coca-Cola.

ADVERTISEMENT

Thar She Blows!

On July 19, 1994, Susan Montgomery Williams of Fresno, California, set a world record for the biggest bubblegum bubble. It was nearly 2 feet wide! Imagine that you blew a huge bubble and floated up into the air like a hot air balloon. What distant place might you visit? Write a bubblegum bubble adventure tale.

_____

_____

_____

_____

_____

_____

_____

_____

_____

_____

_____

_____

_____

_____

_____

_____

The Cheetah and the Sloth

The cheetah is the world's fastest land mammal. It can reach speeds of 65 miles per hour. The world's slowest land mammal is the sloth, which moves along at just .07 miles per hour. That means it would take a sloth 15 minutes just to cross the street. Write a story about a race between a cheetah and a sloth, kind of a wacky version of the old fable, "The Tortoise and the Hare." Here's the twist: Use your imagination to dream up a way for the sloth to win. For example, you could have the cheetah disqualified for cheating.

_____

_____

_____

_____

_____

_____

_____

_____

_____

_____

_____

_____

_____

_____

On the Cover of *Super Star* ☆

Rock star Mick Jagger holds the record for most times on the cover of *Rolling Stone* magazine. He was featured 16 times! Pretend you're the editor of a music magazine called *Super Star*. Pick out a favorite musical act to feature on the cover—it can be Britney Spears, the Backstreet Boys, or whomever you choose. Now, write a story for *Super Star* about your cover subject.

_____

_____

_____

_____

_____

_____

_____

_____

_____

_____

_____

_____

_____

_____

_____

_____

Go for the Gold ☆

Larissa Latynina won 18 Olympic medals, the most ever. This Soviet gymnast competed from 1956 to 1964 and won nine gold medals, five silver, and four bronze. What's your favorite Olympic event: swimming, skiing, pole vault? Pretend that you're a fierce competitor like Larissa Latynina and write a sports story about your performance at the Olympics.

| Volume XIX | # The Olympic Herald | Priceless |

_____

Put your headline here.

_____

_____

_____

_____

_____

_____

Draw a picture to go with your story here.

_____

_____

_____

_____

_____

_____

_____

Virginia Is for Presidents

uess what? The state of Virginia is the birthplace of the most U.S. presidents. Eight presidents have been born there: George Washington, Thomas Jefferson, James Madison, James Monroe, William Henry Harrison, John Tyler, Zachary Taylor, and Woodrow Wilson. Choose one of these Virginia-born presidents and research him. Then write about your president's life and notable accomplishments.

_____

_____

_____

_____

_____

_____

_____

_____

_____

_____

_____

_____

_____

_____

_____

_____

_____

RoboVacuum

The world's smartest robotic vacuum cleaner can be programmed to clean a house all by itself. It has 50 different sensors to make sure it doesn't bump into the wall or run over the cat. What if you could invent your own robot to make life easier? What would it be: a robot lawnmower, maybe, or one that could clean your room? Write about your robotic invention.

_____

_____

_____

_____

_____

_____

_____

_____

_____

_____

_____

_____

_____

_____

_____

Name: _____ **Date:** _____

Fun with Tunnels

The world's longest underwater tunnel stretches for 33.4 miles. It connects Japan with an island called Hokkaido. Construction on the tunnel began in 1964 and wasn't completed until 1988. What if you could build your own tunnel? What kind would it be? For example, you could build a tunnel connecting your house to a friend's house or your house to your school. What would be the advantages of the tunnel? Now, write a story about a tunnel of your own design.

_____
_____
_____
_____
_____
_____
_____
_____
_____
_____
_____
_____
_____
_____
_____
_____

Natural Wonder Land

The world is full of natural wonders. Mount Everest is the biggest mountain, standing 29,035 feet tall. The Grand Canyon is the largest canyon—277 miles long. Dream up an imaginary nation full of natural wonders: volcanoes, deserts, waterfalls, and caverns. Describe some of your country's wonders and give them cool names such as "Splish-Splash Falls." Draw a map, too.

Draw your map here.

The Quick and the Odd

Ashrita Furman of Jamaica is the world's fastest sack racer. Holland's Roy Luiking is the fastest stilt-walker. America's Mark Kenny is quickest at walking using his hands. Imagine that you are a television sports announcer and you are covering a race featuring these three strange speedsters. Describe the action. This will help get you started: "Ladies and gentleman, it's a great day for a race. Today, we have three of the oddest racers . . ."

_____

_____

_____

_____

_____

_____

_____

_____

_____

_____

_____

_____

_____

_____

_____

Adventures of Ultra-Stretch Man and Elasto-Woman

Pierre Beauchemin from France holds the world record for being the most elastic man.

He can twist his body into all kinds of weird pretzel-like shapes. Sounds like a superhero, right? Imagine there was an Ultra-Stretch Man or Elasto-Woman. Write an adventure featuring this super hero.

_____
_____
_____
_____
_____
_____
_____
_____
_____
_____
_____
_____
_____
_____
_____
_____
_____
_____

Name: _____   **Date:** _____

MyLife.com

The most popular web site of all time was **france98.com**. It was a special site created when France was playing in the World Cup soccer tournament. More than one billion people visited this site. Use the space below to create your own personal web site. Fill it with useful information about your school, your home town, hobbies, favorite sports, favorite songs, and anything else you think people will find interesting.

CoolSoft 2.0

Roy Narunksy from Israel holds the world record for youngest software developer. He was just 13 years old when he created a program called Curtains 95 that helps kids run Microsoft Windows on their computers. If you could create a software program, what would it do? Would it be a game or a program that helps kids with math homework, or a special kind of e-mail? Write about your invention and make sure to give it an awesome name like CoolSoft 2.0.

_____

_____

_____

_____

_____

_____

_____

_____

_____

_____

_____

_____

_____

_____

_____

_____

Hamlet the Traveling Cat

amlet is the name of the world's most well-traveled cat. Hamlet escaped from his cage during a flight from Toronto, Canada. Before he was found, he traveled 600,000 miles on an airplane. That's quite an adventure! Write a story about a traveling cat or dog.

_____

_____

_____

_____

_____

_____

_____

_____

_____

_____

_____

_____

_____

_____

_____

_____

_____

_____

Chilly Inn ☆

The Ice Hotel in the Swedish town of Jukkasjärvi is the world's biggest igloo. It can house 150 guests at a time. What if you opened your own igloo hotel? What types of features would you have: cable TV, fine dining, hot bubble baths? Give your hotel a name like Chilly Inn. Then, create a brochure that will make people want to stay in your igloo hotel.

Name of your hotel here.

_____
_____
_____

Draw a picture of your hotel here.

_____
_____
_____
_____
_____
_____
_____
_____
_____
_____
_____

World's Silliest Record

Ray Macareg holds the record for blowing the most bubbles while holding a tarantula in his mouth. He blew 99 bubbles! This may also be the silliest world record of all time. But see if you can come up with an even sillier one. Really stretch your imagination. Then write a newspaper story about the silliest record of all time. What would the headline be?

Volume XIX	# The Super Silly Scoop	Priceless

_____

Put your headline here.

_____

_____

_____

_____

_____

Draw a picture to go with your story here.

_____   _____

_____   _____

_____   _____

_____   _____

_____   _____

_____   _____

Name: _____ **Date:** _____

_____

_____

_____

_____

_____

_____

_____

_____

_____

_____

_____

_____

_____

_____

_____

_____

_____

_____

_____

_____

_____

_____